NACHO
AND
LOLITA

by
PAM MUÑOZ RYAN

illustrated by
CLAUDIA RUEDA

SCHOLASTIC PRESS
NEW YORK

A serenade of thanks to my fellow authors, Robert San Souci and Tony Johnston, for their generous assistance with my research. And to Armando Ramirez for his discovery of the elusive pitacoche.

As always, my gratitude to editors Tracy Mack and Leslie Budnick, and to art director Marijka Kostiw.

—P. M. R.

Text copyright © 2005 by Pam Muñoz Ryan
Illustrations copyright © 2005 by Claudia Rueda
All rights reserved. Published by Scholastic Press, an imprint of Scholastic Inc., *Publishers since 1920.*
SCHOLASTIC, SCHOLASTIC PRESS, and associated logos are trademarks and/or registered trademarks of Scholastic Inc.

LIBRARY OF CONGRESS CATALOGING-IN-PUBLICATION DATA

Ryan, Pam Muñoz.
Nacho and Lolita / by Pam Muñoz Ryan; illustrated by Claudia Rueda.—1st ed.   p. cm.
Summary: A very rare *pitacoche* bird falls in love with a swallow and plucks his colorful feathers to transform dry, barren San Juan Capistrano into a haven of flowers and flowing water, which the swallows can easily find when returning from their annual migration.

ISBN 0-439-26968-7 (hardcover)

[1. Folklore—Mexico. 2. Swallows—Folklore. 3. San Juan Capistrano (Calif.)—Folklore.]
I. Rueda, Claudia, ill. II. Title. PZ8.1.R895Nac 2005. [398.2]—dc22 2004000793

10 9 8 7 6 5 4 3 2 1   05 06 07 08

Printed in Singapore   46
First edition, October 2005

The text type was set in 13-point Perpetua. The display type was set in Gypsy Switch JF.
The artwork was created using colored pencils.
Book design by Marijka Kostiw

TO

MATTHEW SEAN RYAN

— P. M. R.

TO JORGE,

FOR HOLDING MY HAND

— C. R.

ONCE, when the two Californias ran *alta y baja*, high and low along the sea of the Pacific, a mysterious bird landed on the branch of a mesquite tree in the valley of San Juan. His name was Nacho and he was a *pitacoche*. Rare and majestic, he heralded the sunset with whistling songs and carried the colors of the world in his feathers.

From his perch on the edge of the churchyard, Nacho could see the panorama. Acres of dirt rolled into thirsty riverbeds that held only a trickle of water. Nothing grew in the fields. Even the leaves of the mesquite tree matched the adobe of the Mission San Juan Capistrano.

What a dismal place, Nacho thought.

Everything seemed to blend into the same brown landscape . . .

. . . except for Nacho.

With a little too much pride, he spread his feathers, preening and fluffing

as he waited for the day to fade. Then, at the moment the sun closed

its eye, Nacho trumpeted the passing of the light with song, his trill like

a mysterious wind.

"OO EEE AHHH OOO EEEEE OOOO."

A crowd gathered to admire his evening ritual. "He is so beautiful and his

call is so haunting. He must be a spirit from the past," someone whispered.

"Or a prophet of the future," said another.

Nacho knew the truth. He was the only *pitacoche* for thousands of miles and

hundreds of years. His brilliance sometimes brought him attention. But what

good was it when he had no other bird with whom to share his joy?

The busy churchyard was a pleasant change from Nacho's lonesome travels. He watched people prepare for the March feast of St. Joseph. He listened to the talk about the return of *las golondrinas*, the swallows, and the more he heard, the more curious he became.

"It is a miracle," said one man. "Every year the tiny birds cross the great waters to this very place, arriving on the feast day. Then, when the days grow shorter, they leave again for another world, always together. *¡Una familia fantástica!*"

How romantic, thought Nacho.

The swallows were everything he was not. They were small and strong. He was big and bound to the land, unable to fly long distances without resting. They were a fantastic family flying together over the ocean. He didn't belong to anyone.

Intrigued by the people's preparations and caught up in their enthusiasm, Nacho wondered what *he* could do to help?

I have nothing to offer, he thought, except my songs.

On the feast day, Nacho woke to the clanging of bells. People ran into the churchyard and pointed skyward.

"*¡Las golondrinas!*" they cried.

A scout swallow circled above, then another, followed by a flight of swallows trailing in the sky. All morning they came, swooping down toward the mission and landing in the eaves.

One small swallow chose the belfry of the chapel to make her nest. All day, she flew back and forth to the riverbed, gathering bits of mud and twigs. Each time she passed Nacho, she peeked at him.

Did she notice my glorious feathers? he wondered. My regal stature? I *am* colorful and noble. Or was it something else? Could she see my pitiful and lonely spirit?

As the small swallow made her last trip of the day, the sun said good night and Nacho began *un arullo*, a lullaby.

Every swallow leaned forward to hear the magnificent serenade. The small one stopped on the ox cart and listened.

When Nacho finished his song, he plucked one of his feathers and flew to the ox cart. As was his destiny, once a colorful feather was spent, a gray feather grew back in its place. But Nacho didn't mind. When the swallow took it in her beak, by the mystery of the ages, it became a blue hibiscus.

"What is your name?" Nacho asked.

"Lolita," she said, her cheeks blushing the faintest pink.

"LOW-LEEEEE-TAH, LOW-LEEEEE-TAH,"

he repeated, and his voice filled with notes he had never dreamed of singing.

Days passed and Nacho cheerfully busied himself among the swallows.

He carried bits of dry grass and dollops of mud to their nests, especially Lolita's.

After the speckled eggs appeared, he used his wide wings to protect them, especially Lolita's.

When the chicks were born, he searched for beetles, flies, and spiders, and delivered them to each home, especially Lolita's.

"Thank you, Nacho," she said. "You are splendid. You are magnificent!"

Nacho's bright feathers fluffed, and his heart felt as cozy as the warming breezes.

Every evening, his lullaby echoed throughout the mission.

"LOW-LEEEEE-TAH, OOO EEEEE OOOOO."

By summertime, Lolita and her chicks were always by Nacho's side. Nacho was so full with affection and purpose that he could not remember a time before he came to the mission.

Together, he and Lolita watched the chicks fledge and fly. As the days grew longer, they stayed in the fields until sunset, foraging for worms and bugs.

Then one day, a September gust brought a message with the wind, and a hint of uneasiness settled among the swallows.

"I'm afraid we must leave soon," Lolita reminded him. "And now there is talk that we will never come back here again. The water is drying up. We need mud to make our nests. We need flowers and trees to attract insects, so there will be enough food. Without the river to guide us, we will easily miss this spot next year."

Nacho panicked. He'd forgotten that Lolita would have to leave. Now she might never return.

"Stay with me," he pleaded.

"It's too cold here in the winter. I must migrate or I will die. *You* come with me," she begged. "You would love it in the south Americas. Rivers overflow the banks, flowers decorate the fields . . ." Lolita looked toward the ocean, as if she couldn't wait to cross it, ". . . and the sunsets are the color of papayas."

Nacho hung his head. "I can't fly that far," he said sadly. "I am too big."

"I've asked the others," said Lolita. "There is one idea that might work, if you are willing."

Lolita led Nacho to a quiet cove.

"Carry this branch in your talons," she said. "Fly as long as you can. When you grow tired, drop the branch into the water and rest on it. Then wait for your strength to return so you can fly again."

Nacho did as Lolita instructed and bobbed safely on the calm water.

He practiced every day until the October morning when the scout swallows left and the others prepared to follow.

Could he really go with them? Just the chance made him feel as if he could fly forever.

At last, the time had come to leave the mission. Nacho and Lolita hurried

to a cliff's edge, facing the vast ocean. Nacho gripped the branch. The breeze

lifted him and he followed Lolita over the rough open sea. But after a very short

distance, Nacho was exhausted. He dropped the branch and landed on it just

as he'd practiced. Lolita circled above, waiting for him.

Before Nacho was ready to fly again, choppy waves rocked him from

his perch.

He splashed and struggled and began to sink.

"Nacho! Nacho!" cried Lolita.

He slipped farther and farther beneath the swells.

A thousand swallows turned back, flew down, and lifted Nacho to safety.

On the clifftop, gasping for air, he knew the truth. A big *pitacoche* and a

small swallow were not meant to be together.

"Go," he told Lolita. "We will meet in our dreams."

When she disappeared from sight, his heart felt as barren as the land.

That night as the sun slid away, Nacho's song ached with sadness.

"LOW-LEEEEE-TAH, I LOOOOVE YOU."

Winter came with heavy fog. Nacho sat sentry in the mesquite tree and remembered the happy times with *la familia fantástica*.

He thought about the first time he saw Lolita and how he had given her one of his feathers. He looked at the gray feather that had grown back in its place.

I would give all of my colorful feathers if the swallows and my Lolita would come back, he thought. Wasn't there some way to guarantee their return?

Nacho flew to the belfry every day. The blue hibiscus had taken root among the mud nests and even though the flowers were gone, the strong vine wove its way through the tower, exactly as Lolita had done to his heart.

When spring poked its head into February, the vine held buds that promised returning blossoms. All that from one feather.

Suddenly, Nacho knew what he must do.

In March, when the people began their preparations for the feast of St. Joseph, Nacho began to prepare, too.

He flew to the fields, plucked his orange and yellow feathers, and as fast as he planted them, the acres bloomed with poppies and mustard. He left a trail of blue feathers in the riverbed and it overflowed, filling the small creeks and marshes. He pushed green feathers into the soil until palms danced in the breeze and orange trees flourished. He tucked feathers over arches and balconies, and draperies of bougainvillea appeared.

As Nacho worked, he wondered if the swallows would find their way. Determined, he planted feathers in every patch of earth in the churchyard until a splendor burst forth.

Nacho had used every feather, except one.

When the hallowed bells rang as if they'd never rung before, Nacho searched the sky for Lolita. A million thoughts raced through his mind. What if she doesn't recognize me? What if she doesn't like me now that I'm as drab as a mud hen?

Nacho watched the scout swallows dive around the mission in a frenzy of joy and excitement. One after another they came, followed by a flurry of swallows. He turned his head toward the heavens and waited.

When at last Lolita found Nacho in the mesquite tree, it was as if they'd

been together for thousands of miles and hundreds of years.

"I no longer have my beautiful colors," he said.

"To me, you will always be splendid," she said.

Together, they flew toward the river to gather mud and twigs to make

a nest.

Before the day faded, Nacho plucked the last bright feather from his wing

and tossed it toward the westward clouds.

Then, at the moment the sun closed its eye, Nacho heralded the passing

of the day with a concert . . .

. . . against a papaya sky.

AUTHOR'S NOTE

A few years ago, I began searching for the origins of a folktale I remembered about two mythical birds, a big bird and a little bird who fall in love. Had I first heard the story from my Mexican grandmother? Or read it in a book as a young girl? I didn't know. As I reread folk stories, nothing seemed to fit my memory. Finally, I came upon *A Tale of Love* in the book *Mexican Folk Tales* by Anthony John Campos (University of Arizona Press). Like many stories that are recorded from the oral tradition, Mr. Campos's spare tale was familiar, yet some parts were very different from the version I recalled. One point in particular, though, intrigued me. He referred to the big bird as a *pitacochi* (also known as a *pitacoche,* the spelling I chose to use throughout this book), a word I'd never heard before. It propelled me on a journey to define this unique bird.

While researching, I discovered that *pich* is Mayan for a small bird common in the Yucatán. Only one bird of the flock sings at a time. Was a *pitacoche* a soloist or a diva? During the time of the Incas in Peru, there was a chief named Naymlap who had an entourage of eight officers, including his trumpeter and singer, *Pitazofi*. Was a *pitacoche* an announcer? In the Nahuatl language, *pita* means "to blow on wind instruments," and *cochi* means "to sleep." In Spanish, the verb *pitar* means to whistle. Did the *pitacoche* sing the world into slumber?

I embraced all of these ideas and embarked on my own *pitacoche* creation. The story and plot began to take wing, through my imagination. The names, Nacho and Lolita, were my fancy, as was the device of Nacho carrying the colors of the world in his feathers. When I needed a way for Lolita to return to Nacho, I chose the magical transformation from feather to splendor to alert the swallows, like the age-old custom of leaving a candle in a window for someone you love. (Nacho's sweetheart *had* to be lured back to the ancient and romantic mission!)

Built in 1776-77, the adobe Serra Chapel section of the Mission San Juan Capistrano is the oldest building in California still in use today. For centuries, the mission, which is located near two rivers, had been the ideal location for cliff swallows to build their mud nests. On or near March 19 each year, the swallows arrived in the area from Argentina, approximately 7,500 miles away, to fiestas, parades, and the ringing of bells. However, due to land development and the subsequent reduction in the number of insects, the swallows now spread out to other parts of the county. Still, the tradition of celebrating their miraculous journey remains part of San Juan Capistrano's history and pride.

After this story was written, I mentioned the mysterious *pitacoche* to a librarian, Armando Ramirez. He asked his Mexican mother about the bird and she told me that it was a real bird! After all of my interpretation and research, *Cuitlacoche Común*, also known as a *pitacoche*, is a curved-bill thrasher, a relative of the mockingbird. Does this common bird have the exotic history and ancient powers that I gave to Nacho? In the part of my mind that wishes to believe in folklore, romance, and magic, I say yes. I hope you agree.